RED BIRD DANCED

ALSO BY DAWN QUIGLEY

CHAPTER BOOKS

Jo Jo Makoons: The Used-to-Be Best Friend

Jo Jo Makoons: Fancy Pants

Jo Jo Makoons: Snow Day

FOR TEENS

Apple in the Middle

DAWN QUIGLEY

RED BIRD DANCED

Heartdrum
An Imprint of HarperCollins Publishers

Heartdrum is an imprint of HarperCollins Publishers.

Red Bird Danced
Text copyright © 2024 by Dawn Quigley
Interior art © 2024 by Carla Joseph

Library of Congress Control Number: 2023943539
ISBN 978-0-06-322362-2

Typography by Laura Mock
24 25 26 27 28 LBC 5 4 3 2 1
First Edition

To my big brother, Mike,
who taught me how to ride a bike,
how to catch and hit a baseball, and, more recently,
how to love our kids but let them fly.

RED BIRD DANCED

Bineshiinh, a bird,
    on wings,
    clothed in Creator's colors,
flies in tune
with
the
seasons.

Bineshiinh, a bird,
    teaches the Ojibwe, and teaches us all,
the rhythms and flights
    of life, of hope, and sometimes even   of death.

Autumn guides some birds south
    for protection from harsh conditions.
    Meadowlark whistles memories
        as it journeys away.

Winter blankets the
    birds who stay.
    Chickadee flies
    with

    feathers fluffed,
    insulated from the cold.

Spring calls some birds
    back home.
        Robin reminds us
        life   will   return.
    Hope will return
        again.

Summer welcomes new little ones.
    Cardinals, both red and brown,
    braid their nests that hold their babies
        with melody and story
            until they fly away.

Bineshiinh, a bird,
    shows us that
    an empty nest still holds the echoes
    of the songs it once heard.

THE DANCE
Ariel

I know
      I know
            we can't
            afford them.

      My girl,
      we need money for rent and the search for her, for
                              Auntie Bineshiinh,
but
      there's enough for
      one
      more
      lesson.

Only they are not just   lessons
to me.
They teach and train
my feet
      to hover   above   the ground,
shaking off
harm
and hurt,
      flying   in   hope.

This is the   dance
of my heart.

I love to
use my body to
speak how I feel.
It seems like,
since

                                              Auntie
                                              has
                                              gone
                                              missing,

they
look right
through me,
looking for   Auntie.

Do they
see
my heart
when I
pirouette?

I'M UP
Tomah

ISeeMyTurnComingUp
Page 4   Page 7   Page 11

    You're up, Tomah.

I do not see the puzzle on the page
    like they do.
I do not connect the chaos.
I do not link the letters.

Only
    black
        blots
                mocking
                        me.

    You're up, Tomah. Page 13.

It is dagwaagin, autumn.
And   I   am   back   here   again.

Hmmm? Oh.
    OhNoOhNoOhNo.

Okay, Ms. Begay—I inhale too quickly:

cough

cough

cough.

And, also, my chili burrito lunch is making its way out.

EWWW! Tomah's gonna cough up a hair ball!
Ha
Ha
PHEW, Tomah's gonna fart!
Ha
HA

All right, all right, Mr. Tomah, go get some water, and
we'll just

move   on   to   the   next   person
to read.

I
can't
wait
to
get
back
home.

Making jokes is how I escape
getting caught.

Laughter buys
    me
         time.

Time
until
I can
exhale
again.

UntilTomorrow.

ONE LESS
Ariel

I live in
the
Intertribal
Housing
Complex
with
my
mom,
baby
brother,
and
not   my   Auntie Bineshiinh
                                                                    anymore.

Dagwaagin guides the leaves falling
    Down
        Down
                Down.   Stories buried in each leaf.

I just want to
make my
mama
smile   again,

but her smile is lost
  until we find

              Auntie.

BOLD WORDS

Tomah

I always carry a plastic bag with me in my pocket when I
walk around the quad. To pick up trash.
After a storm, there is sometimes

g a r b a g e
everywhere.

Today I walk past the projects' rental office. Crumpled by
the front door are flyers.

VACANCIES AVAILABLE NOW!

Why not rent one of our fifty town houses in the metro's
Native American Intertribal Housing Complex? How **does
living** in a community with over 300 tribal residents sound?
Our 12-acre community has green play areas, off-street
parking, and youth and Elder care, along **with** rent support.
We are one of the largest urban Native American Section 8
subsidized housing **communities** with financial **aid**
provided in **the heart** of the city. Located within the Indig-
enous Cultural Corridor, we are **close to** Native American
Family Center, Indian Health Services, bus lines, 3 Sisters'
Healing Garden, and Directions Elementary School.
Questions? Please call for tours.

Aaniin, Tomah!
        Tomah, I'm bringing your family soup tonight!

Living here
in my Native community
heals my
heart,

mostly.

ROOTS ENTWINED
Ariel

Life in the housing complex
means
family is a
doorstep away.
Life is in
our relatives,
relatives
who may not
be blood related
    but are like tree
    roots that
        intertwine and hold on
        to one another unseen.
A
single feather
can do nothing.
But huddling
together, on a bird,
feathers hold
and take
flight.

BENCHED
Tomah

I sit all
by
myself
on
the
bench
outside
the
front door.
Some
people
might
think
where
I live
is
old,
run-down,
with graffiti-covered walls,
weeds peeking between pavement,
and lots of
noise.
But we,

Ariel and I,
always smile
when we say,

                    We're home.

This
morning,   my   friend
Ariel
waves
to
me
across
the
quad.
I
think
of
her
like
a
cousin:
always see her,
always together,
always, she smiles back.

Her
long
black
hair
matches
the
black
birds'
feathers.

Ariel
is
eleven years old
but is so smart.

We
are
in the

         same grade.
       But I am twelve.

I
had
to

repeat repeat repeat repeat repeat repeat repeat repeat
repeat
third grade.

She
walks
with
her
mama
to
the
tribal
daycare.
Her
mama
watches
our
projects'
little ones.

Ariel
always
smiles at me.
Even when nobody
else does.

It is the only smile
    I
        have
           seen
              today.

A smile is the   s   u   n.

And I am the r
                a
                i
                n.

PIROUETTE PAST
Ariel

See my toes
                    float
                              above
                                        this all?

See my family
watch
me with
        pride
as   I   try to pirouette
                    past our hurt hearts?

          I know, my girl, I know.
          Just enjoy your
                    last   lesson   today.

To dance
is
to dream
and
to find
smiles again and
to think past an empty smile and
          empty   laughter.

And an   empty   chair.

How will my body
speak through
dance again?

I can dance
so they
smile with hope,

w
    a
       i
         t
           i
             n
               g

                    for

                              Auntie.

I GET
Tomah

See how well your neighbors do in

school?

Why
can't
you
do
the
same? Dad says as he
walks out the door
to his security
job.

Art, I get.
Math, I get.
MusicAndGymAndSports,
I get.
Waiting
for
Mama
to braid
my and my dad's
hair
into
a

single
braid
in the
morning,
I get.
Daddy nodding
to me
when he
leaves for
work,
I get.

When
    I
        look
back   and
forth
      at   the   letters,
all   I   see
  is fear.

        Fear of being found out.

        Fear of being made fun of.

        Fear of being left behind
           alone.

Alone, like the
     l a s t
dried leaf   hanging on the branch. Alone.

SHADES OF SHADOWS
Ariel

See how pretty
Auntie is?

See how
Mama
   keeps
                                    Auntie Bineshiinh's
picture
      by her chair?

See, Mama,
   how I drew my best picture
for
you?

                                      Auntie

taught me to draw.
Taught me how to
   shade the colors
      for even brighter light.

  Oh, look, you used
  my favorite colors, my girl.

I wait to see it.
But
no smile today.

I go back to
my schoolwork project:
"Name a problem, and
find a   solution."
I know the problem, but
                    not
                            the
                    solution

                                    yet.

                                    Play? Now?

My baby brother,
Misko, asks again.
Smiling up at
me.
No, not now, baby.

Mama says to me,

Ariel, why don't you go out to
play on the grass? Before it gets dark.
But it's so dark
                    in   here.

And so
I step out the front door,
        but there is
                no
                        light outside either.

INVISIBLE BIRD
Tomah

See
Mama
Cardinal?

See
her dance
to the beat
of the wind?

She
is
                invisible.

No
one
notices
what
she
does.

I

    think

       I

          must be

            a brown cardinal,

               too.

                  And am   invisible.

But sometimes,
that's
exactly
    what   I   want.

Especially
    at

        school.
        Tomah, Ms. Begay always says to me quietly,
        why do you try to hide behind your jokes?
        You have so much to say.

My
teacher
doesn't
know
what

I'm
h i d i n g
from.
Jokes keep the truth
      a   w   a   y.
But
it's
always
t h e r e.
Instead I say,
Aww, Ms. Begay,
my humor is the
best part
of my Native charms!

DANCING FOR HOPE
Ariel

Each of my
Turtle Mountain
Ojibwe
relatives
    says   over
        and   over
             and   over,
    My girl, keep dancing for us;
    dance for those who
    cannot dance anymore.
    But in our way, our healing way.
    Jingle dancing, Ariel.

But my ballet?
What   about   that?
I've danced ballet for most of my life.
How will I speak with the music?
I wish
my
voice
was louder.

Mama says,
Too expensive, still, my girl.
What about dancing for us?

Ariel,
our community
needs healing.
Our community
needs hope.
Our community
needs

                    you.

                              Will you, our girl,
                              dance in our way,
                                   as a jingle dress dancer?
                                   We need
                                   you.
                                   We need
                                   healing.

Could it be
the
same?

Could one
dance
take the place
of another?

EACH
Tomah

Each building,
like my own
in the Intertribal Housing Complex,
has a name:
    Fontain, Wambdi, Ogimaa, Four Bears, and more.

Ariel and I have lived
here
our
whole
lives.
Her   auntie

used
to
babysit
us
every
summer.

Ayy, you two
could be siblings!
But, Tomah, you
have

better
eyelashes.

Ha ha
　　ha ha!

But, Auntie,
what do
I have?

Well, you, Ariel,
have
the darkest brown eyes
that
shine
like a
beautiful
old soul's.
And
although
you barely
reach
my shoulder,
you
are
mighty.

She
taught
us how
to see

p   a   s   t

what
others might
see.
And
she
taught
us how
to
draw
birds.

Add more wings, kids,
when you draw bineshiinyag!
Each feather tells of what
they see.
Each feather is a story.
Let the words fly!

More than a thousand people
    from over twenty-five tribal Nations live here.
Across the two square miles of land
where we
    live
    and
    teach
and
    don't learn
how
they, the city schools,
say learning is done.
    My dad and Elders say,
    My boy, Tomah, come listen.
    Come listen like
        only
            you
                can
                    do.

Listening, I read the songs, stories, and teachings
    of the Elders.
    I read the words
    in my ears
    and heart.

In them,
as biboon arrives soon with snow,
in their stories,
I feel

able to learn

in our Indigenous way.

HIDING HEARTS
Ariel

Each time in school
I
hold my breath
for my good friend
Tomah as he
    tries to hide.

He can't
hide his outside;
he has big
shoulders
and is almost
six feet tall.

But he tries to
hide
    his inside.

We always used
    to play

                          hide and

seek
with

the other
kids.

I also know what
it
        means
                to   hide
                in school.

I can hide
because of my
        sadness;   missing

                                    my   Auntie Bineshiinh

        clouds who can see me.
                                I am invisible.

All around me I hear questions . . .

        When is the last time anyone saw her?
            Who was she with?
                    When did she last answer her cell phone?
        Why aren't they doing anything to

                                            find her?

At school,
we are working
on a
current events
assignment:
Name a problem, and find a solution.

Some students
choose
football | pollution | equality | lunch nutrition.

But I
choose

                                        #MMIW.
                                        #Missing
                                        and
                                        Murdered
                                        Indigenous
                                        Women.

        Problem: Native American women and girls
            are going   *missing.*

        Solution: I don't know, but our
            voices can shed light on this   *darkness.*
Tomah looked at me
and nodded.

Ariel,
it's good
to learn
how to
help
when
our
Native
SistersMothersDaughters
are   *missing.*

LOOK UP
Tomah

Each
finch,
each
cardinal,
each
mourning dove,
here
knows
how
to

                fly.

But
why

                can't
                I?

Where   can I
                belong
                in the
                sky?

Tomah, Ms. Begay always says,
why don't you look up from
    that same page
      you've been
        staring at?

I
can
look

       p
     u

and
see
my
teacher
gaze
at
me
with
her
kind
eyes.

Eyes
the
same
color
as
a
mama
cardinal's.

ANCESTORS' WAYS
Ariel

> *Ancestors' ways*
> *of honoring*
> *our women*
> *somehow*
> *I think*
> *got*
>
>   *lost,*
>
> says Mama.

I wonder
   how   can   I
honor my
ancestors
by
finding
my
mama's
smile
again.

Because the ancestors'

      s

         t

            e

                p

                   s

still   echo
on every
piece of
land
in
what
we
now
call
    the United States.

Sometimes
    at   summer   powwows
    I can feel
        their vibrations.

Dancing is how I connect
    my body
    and soul
    to the earth.

How will I do this now?
No more ballet.
Yet
             my feet   **do not**
                feel
                        lost.

Can my dance
be done
another
    way?

I *wonder,*
does the earth
feel the steps
of

                              Auntie?

SNOW KISSED THE GROUND
Tomah

Ancestors' stories
were told
only when
snow
    kissed the ground.

Ariel's   auntie
used to tell
us stories in biboon, winter.

My boy,
in biboon,
come winter,
come listen,
come learn
to tell
our stories.

But, I asked,
how does
the snow
carry the
stories?

Tomah, each story has its own
wings
that spread
out, showing
each
feather.

Ancestors'
ways
of knowing
are
not
like
now.
Each
time
a
new
person
meets
me,
they
usually
say
the
same
thing.

You're a big
one,
aren't you?

    Tall for your
    age,
    aren't you?

        Liked third grade so much
        you did it twice!

        But you
        sure are
        slow,
        aren't you?

I
don't
know
what
that
means,
but
maybe
I
am
slow.

Slow
to
get
angry.
    I slow
    down
    to
    watch
    the
    birds
        and everyone.

    I slow
    down
    to
    sit
    and
    remember
    how
    the
    ancestors
    lived
    to
    protect
        each   other.

If only my Elders
could be my
teachers, too.

Then I could
stand proud.
          And not

                                        have to
                                   hideAtSchool.

SPACE BETWEEN EARTH AND SKY
Ariel

Light,
light,
that's how
I feel
when
my feet

earth.

the

leave

Ariel,
you
dance
so
good,
Tomah says.

He's older than I am,
bigger
in a

way
that makes you
feel
so
safe.

    Safe to
    walk across
    the quad
    from the
    front door
    to my other
    relatives' and friends' houses
    in the
    projects.

        Sometimes there are bad things
        that go on outside
        my front door in the city:
        drugs,
        muggings,
        graffiti,
        and even missing   people.

        And it
        scares me.

But Tomah
sits on the bench
outside the front door,
each season,
watching the birds,

    but really,
    I think,
        watching out for us all.

    Ariel, how is your research
    project?

Good, Tomah, good.
Sad, but . . .
it's something
I can do.
Do instead of just
            waiting for

                        Auntie.

I walk inside. Mama looks
           up.

Light the candle,
my girl.
Put it in the window.
    Might help
    her find her way

                                                home.

Little Misko reaches for me.

                      Up?

Let's play later, Misko.
Let's play later, Misko.
Let's play later, Misko.
Let's play later, Misko.
Let's play later, Misko.

It's getting lighter
each day now.
Dawn climbing
from the
dark.

Will the light

find me?

MY MASK
Tomah

Light
　　peeks
　　　　　through
　　　　　　　my
　　　　　　　　　blinds

each
dawn.

But light
isn't bright
enough
　　to shine
　　　　on
the　　　　words
　　　　　　on　　　　the　　　　page.

Last week of November
means biboon is
　　coming.

　　　Tomah, what's up?

At the bus stop.
        Tomah, hey, what's going on?

I put on my face.
My confident mask.
Humor is my
        invisibility cape.

It's
how
I
hide.

Yep, nothing's up,
    except my
    intelligence
    and good looks.

        Ayyyy, Tomah!

Heavy
winds
don't
keep

me
from
sitting
on
my
bench
outside.

I
feed
the
birds.

I wish
I could
hear
the
stories
waiting
on
their
feathers.

Ariel's

Auntie
Bineshiinh

first told me how
birds live together
and [protect] each
other.
And
how
we
can
[protect]
them, too.

Hey, Tomah,
what's up?

Ricky,
my
neighbor,
likes
to
say
hi
to
me
as
he
goes

to
early
basketball
practice
at
school.

Maybe
someday
I
could
be
on
a team
where
people
would
let
me
be
a
part
of
something.

But for now,
    I will sit here
        and watch,
        only watch,
            because my
            heart hurts
            too much to move.

BEAUTIFUL THINGS
Ariel

Breathing
in
    and
        out

in
    and
        out.

My girl,
how wonderful
that Tomah's grandmother
gifted you with this
beautiful
    jingle dress.

Eya, I don't deserve it.
How do I accept beautiful things
when my   auntie's missing?
Yet something deep
is calling me.

My heart can feel
its   vibrations
of   healing
of   love
of   great responsibility.

Ariel, the Elders
see healing in your
          steps when you practice with Tomah's
          grandma.
Each tink *tink tink*
          of the jingles
matters.

I practice
      these new
          jingle dance
             steps
                on the tile floor.

The sound, the movement,
    moves my soul.
         Tink
           tink
             tink.

Maybe it wasn't ballet,
but the sound the
     air made
          as I
               moved through it—
               that I love.

The sound
     of me
          dancing out of   the silent shadows.

But

B
R
E
A
T
H
I
N
G
     is
     something
     I
     think

about
because
    I hope
    my   Auntie Bineshiinh
                                           is
                                         still

                                       breathing.

JUMBLED LETTERS

Tomah

Breathing
in,
breathing
out.

Trying to
make
the   words
magically   make   sense.

Trying
to
breathe
life
into

the   jumbled
letters   skipping
across   the
page.

Ms. Begay, that breakfast sausage
sandwich is speaking
loudly now.
     Can I—
          Oh, Mr. Tomah,
          again? Sure.
          Take the bathroom pass.

               Ugh, gross, Tomah!
               You're doing that on purpose!
               Pee-YOO!

               Ha   ha   ha!

Yep, you found out
my superpower, guys!
I smell as fresh
as commodity cheese
on a hot
summer day.
Deadly smells
only come
from the fiercest
warriors.

Okay, Mr. Comic, Tomah, good luck.
Come back before we start
reading lessons.

Stomach,

thanks   again.

But
    I'm
        running
            out
                of
                    excuses.

#MMIW

Ariel

    Ariel, my grandma says you can come
    over for more
        jingle dance lessons.
Miigwech, Tomah,
      I'll be right over.
I'm working
on my school project.
Mama looks
over my shoulder at my   #MMIW
paper.
And nods.
      It's good to learn
      and grow
      your voice, my girl.

I think
I'm starting
to find
    m y s e l f .

Tomah's grandma
   was a champion
      dancer,
      but she isn't dancing
      anymore.   At least for now.

Until   my Auntie Bineshiinh
is found.
Life is so
different now.
Different

                                   without

Auntie.

And it will never
   be
      the
         same.

READING LIVES
Tomah

> *Life isn't*
> *always what it*
> *seems, Tomah,*
>   *my boy.*

Yes, Grandmother,
I know.
Believe me.
    I know.
Grandma
lives
with
my mom, my dad, and me.
I
can
read
her
face
and
see
how
much
she

misses
my   grandpa.

Now, snow
may be gone soon.
Tell me one of the stories
we've been working on, my boy.
            It is biboon, time for
                        stories.
You make us Fort Peck Assiniboine
people proud to hear you.

Yes, Grandma.
Daddy comes in
from the kitchen to
listen.
I found a feather
today,
and it
told me a story.

There was a bird
who lost its
voice.
No one
had

ever
heard it sing before.
No one
except
the wind.
"Sister Bird,
I will help
you find
your voice again,"
Wind said.

I wish I
could find my
voice, too.

Because   now
            it's   lost
                    to   the
                        pages,
                            letters,
                and
                        words.

But with
my birds
and storytelling,
I

can
take
off
my
invisibility
cape.

And now
there
is
one less
bird
singing
here.

It
makes
my
heart
hurt
even
more.

Even
more
than
usual.

THE KNOCK
Ariel

The knock came
late at night.
That dark, dark night,

after all those weeks.

Mama opened the door.
The police.

"Ma'am, so sorry,

we found

her . . ."

We all held
our
breaths.
Our
breaths,
in and out,

causing the
l   a   s   t
small, brown leaf
to

fall off the tree.

Air
we haven't
exhaled
since
Auntie
went
missing
last
fall.

". . . by the railroad
tracks. Lying
in the snow.
Injuries

leading

to

death.

So sorry to have to tell you
all.
We're collecting evidence to open a
case . . . could be a natural /death/.
B   U   T . . .

She's,
Bineshiinh's, ███."

Officers
walked
back
into the
night.

Darkness is our new
blanket.

INTO
Ariel

Into the
community gathering
space,
we walk
quietly.

Quietly
everyone
hugs and nods
to
my family.

        So sorry . . .
           I will miss Bineshiinh . . .

               Always was smiling . . .

Today, my
feet do
not dance.
The snow
crackles, echoes of   our lost auntie.
    Only my tears
        travel

across

the

air.

Walking on, into the
next world

from this one,
is something
I don't really
understand.

We will watch over her all night,
until dawn emerges . . .
then the ceremony.

Maybe the morning light
will shine
on our
sadness?

Ariel, how are you?
Okay, dumb question.

Thanks, Tomah.
I'm happy

my Turtle Mountain
family
is here now.
But
could you,
Tomah,
since there's snow still
on the ground,
could you tell
a story . . . ?

Well, as you know,
Wind told
Sister Bird,
"I will help
you find
    your voice.
But first you must find
your song."
And so Sister Bird
   flew
      and flew
        and flew.
Trying to find her
   song.

The room gathered; Ms. Begay was there, too.
Everyone stopped
to listen to Tomah, the storyteller.

The song wasn't found in rain.
The song wasn't found in pain.
The song wasn't even found in
        what does not remain.

"Then where, Brother Wind,
where is the song found?"

                    The room waits.

"Sister Bird,
the song is where it has
        always been.
Embedded in your heart,
        your spirit,
        and in all."

                And everyone
                now knows Auntie's song.

It has been here all along.

DANCED ALONE
Tomah

> *. . . Into the kitchen, my boy.*
> *Yes, Tomah, bring the food.*

I help to carry the dishes of
wild rice,
venison,
potatoes,
and
frybread
    to the
      gathering space.
We're here to watch
    and
        protect
            and pray
                for
Ariel's   Auntie Bineshiinh

all night,

                    as she
                  prepares for
                    her journey.

After, I walk home
from Ariel's
auntie's wake
and ceremony.
We
kept
watch
and prayed
all night.

Mama, can I?
Can I . . .
do
something
for
Ariel's   auntie?
I want to do it for
        our missing
        sisters, mothers,
        and
        daughters.
Eya, my boy,
        my Tomah.

My boy, take my red dress.
It symbolizes
our   missing sisters, mothers, and daughters.

Mama, are the empty red dresses

S

     A

           D?

No, my boy,
they remind
us of
our   missing Native sisters, mothers, and daughters—

the ones who never
go missing from our
hearts.

I laid Mama's
red dress,
empty,
on a clothes hanger
and put
it on top
       of a pole
       the projects'
       janitor lent to me.

For once I knew what to do.

I walked around
        and around
        and around
        the projects' quad,
        then left the complex
        for the next block
        and the neighborhood,
        around the streets
        of our city
        world.
The   red dress

    d   a   n   c   e   d   alone

in
the
cold breeze.

It made my
heart hurt
        even more
        than it
                usually did.

Dad
watched from
the sidewalk.
I could
read
the
questions in
his
eyes.

I don't speak smart.
But this red dress,
        empty red dress,
        held high
        says
                        all we need to
                             say
                        about our
                        missing

        AuntiesMamasSistersDaughters.

RED, RED IS CALLING

Ariel

We looked out the window and
saw
Tomah
holding up
the red dress.

It's for our missing and murdered
Indigenous
women.
Too
many
lost.
Too
many
go
without
anyone
looking
into
their
cases.
Empty
dress,
red,
mirroring
the
violence,
but also
the only color
that spirits can
see.
My mama
says that
red,
red
is calling
back
our
missing
Indigenous
women,
calling
their
spirits back, to speak to us, to mingle among us for a while again. And to speak for
their justice.

OUR LAST STEPS
Tomah

Our
last
steps
around
the
blocks
make
a lot
of people
look.
I
don't
know
if
they,
the non-Indians,
understand
what
the

red
dress

means.

I
look
behind
me.
So
many
from
the
housing
projects
and
school
are
following
me.
Even
Daddy's
boss,
Representative Richards,
from the
state
building
walks
behind me.

I
must
not
be
    invisible anymore.

                      Or maybe
                      I just thought
                      I was.

Tomah!
the little ones say as we walk with the red dress.
    Tell us another story!
    Quick, while the snow is still sitting on the ground.

No, not today.
Today's not the day
for fun stories.
    Sad faces
        look back at me.

But let me
tell you one
about a
new song
    Sister Wind just learned.

About how the color
red appeared in the
four sacred colors
        when dawn
        first
        woke.

JINGLE DRESS HEALING
Ariel

Native
jingle   dress
dancing
isn't
ballet.

It's more than
pointe shoes
and tutus
and European composers.

Tink
tink
tink.

Ballet was for
me.
But

jingle dancing
    is
        for
            my
                Native
                community.
And for me, now, too.

        Mama said,
        Ariel, my girl,
        this jingle dress
        dance is
        a powerful
        healing medicine.
        Will you dance for us? Will you dance to heal?

Eya, I will be
honored
    to dance,
    to heal,
        to represent the projects.

I
have
found
my

dancer's
heart
again.

TO BE SMALL
Tomah

Native American Heritage Month
is coming up soon, in May.
In ziigwan.
Everyone will
read from
their essay.
    Onstage.
    After the powwow.
    In front of
    the school
    and the community.
    Ms. Begay asks,
    Tomah,
    will you read
    something?

It'sComingTooSoon.
The   words
     will   run   away
   from   me   as
          usual.
ButInFrontOfEverybodyThisTime.
Usually, I feel
so

B   I   G.

But now I only

wish

to

be

SMALL.

ABOVE THE JINGLES
Ariel

Hearts cover
some of
my jingle dress
    regalia.

Mama asked if
I wanted her to add
    more beads,
    just above the jingles.
        Ariel, what more should I bead?

I don't know—
    how do I choose?

        What speaks to you
        when you dance now?
I can feel
    my heart
        more.
I can feel
    the air and birds, in spring now,
        holding me
            more.

More than ballet?

Eya, Mama.
   I liked ballet,
but my heart beats
     more with the light now
     more with the drum now
     more with the birds in flight
than it ever did before.

Now I *need* to dance,
and before, I just
     wanted to dance.

Mama looked
deep into
my eyes.

Ariel,	Mama,
you	I
must	want to
dance	dance
for	for
yourself.	myself.

We bead and sew,
yet can't ignore
how our house feels
smaller now.
I don't
know how that can
       be
since the heaviness
of our hearts

takes up so much space.

But I know
the jingle dress
      will make the sound
            and help speak
                  in my school project.
For those who   can't speak   anymore.

HEARTS
Tomah

> *Hearts, Tomah,*
> *that's the word.*

Oh, Ms. Begay,
  ItLooksLike
    hats   to me.
          She asked me to stay back at recess.
          Never a good thing.

>   *Tomah, can you look at this sentence on the board?*
Yes, ma'am, looks pretty good to me.

>   *Tomah, you know your dad and I are cousins, right?*
Yeah, so . . .
>   *Well, it means we're family. From back on the Fort*
>   *Peck rez.*
Yeah, Ms. Begay, that's right.
>   *So, you're a gifted storyteller, a comic, Tomah, as we all*
>   *know, and so much more.*
But—
>   *I'd like us to meet after school and practice reading*
>   *using a special method.*
>   *Tomah, I believe*

you might have a reading
         disability.

Ugh, I, I
      IDon'tSeeWhatYouAllSee
                  on   the   page.
         Tomah, you know, it's just a different way of seeing
         letters and words. There are
                  special techniques I can help you with.

Would
you
help
me?
Can
you?
So I might be able
      to
see   what   everyone   else   sees?

      Tomah, would I lie to you?

It depends if we're playing blackjack,
      or if you're being my teacher.

Tomah, it's the rest *of us who wish we could*
see
what and how
you
see in your stories.
Maybe
   I

                               don't
                               have
                               to
                               hide

anymore.

Maybe this
is like how
Native
birds
stay
here
over
the
winter
and
emerge
in ziigwan.
I

think
they
face
the
hard
things
in
life
but
know
they
could
not
live
another way.

MOURNING TOGETHER
Ariel

Together, Mama and I
    stare into her bedroom mirror.

Native ways
of

                                       mourning

are different
    from white people's ways.

Mama

/c   u   t/   her
                              l o n g **hair**.

        It is my deep sadness
        and a reminder on
            my body,
            showing my   *loss.*

Mama /cut/ her
    long hair since
    that was the before time
    with   Auntie.

Now, when it
    grows,
it will be my life
after my   *sister, our Bineshiinh.*

Mama, should I do that?
/Cut/ my hair?

My dear girl,
my sweet Ariel,
so wise beyond your years,
only if one needs to.
    I see you, my girl.
    I see how you
    dance in your way now.
    What a big heart you have.

Only, I wonder, did   Auntie
have to   walk on,
for me

                                   to see myself?

Maybe
I
made
myself
invisible?

BIRDS AND I
Tomah

Together,
the
birds
and I
share
the space
outside the front door.
Green leaves return now,
like my birds.

But my heart
shouldn't
hurt
this much.
I try
to
get up
from
the bench
outside
our building.
But I—
    But I—

I
I
I
I . . .

Tomah!
              What's going on? Why is he on the ground?
         Tomah, are you messing around? Or—
Someone call 911!
                   Tomah, no, no, get *up*!

Feathers
flood
the
grounds.
Sounding
their
silent
alarm.

A SONG FOR MISKO
Ariel

At home, I hear

Riel, play?

I take my brother, Misko,
in my   l a p
and hum
him
a song
my mama
used to
sing to me.

BLANK WALLS
Tomah

> *Son, Tomah?*
> > *My boy, can*
> > *you hear us?*

My eyes
blink
    blink
       blink.

Dad, Mama?
I . . . breathe in
but can't breathe out . . .
> *Son, you're okay;*
> *you're in the hospital.*

> *Oh, Tomah,*
> *you had us so*
> *w o r r i e d !*

I
can
see and hear
my parents,

and I can
read the

> white walls
> white blanket
> white curtains
> white ceiling.

> It reads
> like bleach.

Hospital.
I look
   d   o   w   n
at my chest.
There are
    wiresANDtubesANDbandages.

Mama? What? *? ?*
I'm
scared,
but . . .
but
I
read
calm
on their
faces.

I breathe   out.

Tomah, you collapsed. Everyone ran out.

Grandma called the ambulance.

My boy, Mama says, *you had heart surgery.*

And, son, you did so well. You are a brave boy.

No, a brave warrior who fought for his heart.

All I can hear

is

heart surgery. Heart surgery. Heart **surgery.**

And yet,

for once,

my heart

feels like

it

fits

in

my

chest.

Maybe my

heart

had to

/break/

to

be healed?

BROKEN HEARTS
Ariel

We visit Tomah
in the hospital
   downtown.

We, all the families from our quad, ride
   the
      elevator
      to the

                                top floor.

        The penthouse suite,
           Tomah tells us later.

His room door is
   slightly open.

We knock.
       Biindigaw.

Aaniin, Tomah.
               I ask, Tomah, how you feeling?
He has so many tubes stuck in him.

Tomah seems
so little
   in his bed.
A giant heart
   broken.
I hope it will be made
   whole again.

I will dance for him,
my lifelong friend, Tomah,
just as he has
always been
there for me.

I will dance for him.
   Jingle dance
   for his healing
      at the powwow.

MY BIG HEART
Tomah

We left
the
hospital
after
a week.

> *Enlarged heart, or cardiomegaly, Tomah.*
> *That's why you felt pain*, said the doctor.

Enlarged
means big.
I know
I
have
a
big
heart.
But I
didn't know
it would hurt
  so much.

> Daddy looked at Mom. *Tomah, be sure to*
> *tell us if you're not feeling well.*
> *Don't keep it a secret.*

I have to
take
medicine now.
It
will
make my
heart better.

But
I
hope
my
heart
stays
big.
Big
enough
to keep
my watch
        at the projects.

Ariel said
everyone in
the projects
took turns
feeding my birds.

It was like the feathered ones knew I was gone.

And were keeping watch

    for my return.

PEEKING THROUGH
Ariel

Must be true:
Hearts aren't
broken
    forever.
That's what
my mama
    says.

I keep working on
my school project:
stories
names
dates
of the   missing.
I felt useless,
but now I
can help be a
    v o i c e .

Baby brother, Misko, looks at me:

                          Play?

He giggles and
    snuggles his head in
    Mama's neck.

And little Misko just
    uncovered
    her smile.

I see the sunlight; warmth comes soon,
    peeking through our window shades.

COME TOGETHER
Tomah

Must
be
hard
not to be
    Native.
We have
each other.
We laugh together,
we cry together,
we live together
and
come together
when somebody   walks
                                                     on.

It makes me
think
of my birds.
They live,
    build nests,   and love   together.

They sing their stories.
I sing mine, too.

FEET IN FLIGHT
Ariel

We tell stories

                                        of Auntie.

We tell how

                                        she looked,
                                        laughed,
                                        and loved us

all.

   Remember when Bineshiinh painted the mural over the
graffiti?
            Bineshiinh always had time for us kids!

      She took me to my first powwow.

            Remember when she was the only one who would
      eat my burned frybread?

                                                    auntie
My
bought my first
dance shoes.
She set my
feet in flight.

We tell our stories
for baby brother, Misko,
    and others
so they will remember   Auntie

as she was in life, her
    bright life.

                                        Not how she
                                        was found in
                                        ~~death~~.

                                            Her life
                                            is like

the feathers.
Together,
our love and
memories
bind together,
like feathers,
to fly
and tell

                                        her story.

TOGETHER, WE
Tomah

My teacher
   and I
meet after school
every day.

     Tomah, see?
     You've worked so hard
     and are doing fantastic
     using the reading techniques.

Ziigwan, spring, is here.
Here in the projects
we share many of our languages.
I echo the Ojibwe Elders' words.
(They talk
a lot!)
And now the words are not flying around the page
anymore.
But *I* feel I can fly.
Fly in written stories now, too, just
         like the ones I tell.
Ms. Begay
gave me

a book
about
birds.
Its
words
tell
me
the story.

STEP INTO THE CIRCLE
Ariel

> *Will you dance*
> *with my eagle feather*
> *fan, Ariel?*

Eya, miigwech.
    I
        will
            be
                honored.

It's the end of May,
our state's
Native American Heritage Month.

It's the day of our powwow.

It's my first time
    in public
        jingle dress dancing.

           Tink tink tink.

        We all line up for the Grand Entry.

Tink

tink

tink.

We stand together, with the jingle dress dancers.

Colors vivid.

Beads bright.

Some without fans held aloft.

Some with.

In we step, into the circle,

following the tall eagle staff and our veterans.

Time stops.

The air encircles my feet and legs

as they

step in time,

then double time

to the

drum.

My beaded birds

help me

f   l   y   .

Tomah is sitting in the front bleacher.

In front of him,
    I dance, fan

                                    high.
                         raised

                   Tink
                       tink
                           tink.

Blessing him,
    praying for him,
        honoring him.

I turn the circle, and
                tink
                    tink
                        tink.

Blessing   Auntie,

              praying for her journey,
           honoring her.

And next to me,

in the circle,

a red bird danced.

READY TO FLY
Tomah

Will do!
I'll be there right after
the powwow, Ms. Begay.

I guess I'm going through
with it—
the reading
in public.

Been practicing
for a long time.
I feel good.
I feel strong.
I feel ready to
    fly.

> *Good luck, Tomah.*
> *You'll be very good*
> *reading your essay*
> *   on the emcee's stage.*

Thanks, Ariel.
And, Ariel,

you know, I'm really
    sorry about your Auntie Bineshiinh.

But remember, you
don't need to think
it's up to you
to find your mom's
    smile.
It's not your job
to make people smile.

        Tomah,
            it's not
                  yours either.

Wow.

Then I faked a faint.
    'Cause I knew
        it'd make her laugh.

And it did.

My
heart
felt

so
good
when
    Ariel
jingle danced
    and blessed me and
        prayed for me
at the powwow.

It
is
a good
spring
day.
A
day
of
life
with
our
Native place,
Native stories,
Native community.

AN OJIBWE GIRL
Ariel

Survive.
What does that mean
to me,
an Ojibwe
girl living
in the
        projects?
Surviving,
to me,
is
remembering how
        our ancestors
always worked
in community
        to endure.

Not to be prideful of
a skill,
        like ballet,
but how
        I live my life

to help and dance
    for
        everyone.
            Not   just   me,

    but   us   all.

I finished
my school project about   #MMIW.
But there's
one
more
thing
to
do.

Later that ziigwan afternoon, I hold the phone tightly in my
hand.

        Will you wait, please?

Yes, ma'am.
I can wait to talk
    to
        my
            state representative.

Mama nods at me
from across the room,
wiping sweat from her face.
Not from nerves,
but from the air's warm   breath.

I wrote down what I
    wanted to say.
Because it's about
what happened to   my auntie.

And how this can't happen anymore.

        Hello? Representative Richards is on the line.

Hello, Ms. Richards.
My name is Ariel and I
    live in the
            Intertribal Housing Complex
            in the city.

It's in your district.
My friend
Tomah's
dad
works

at
the
capitol building's
security desk.

Yes, of course, what can I do for you?
I'm so, so very sorry about your   *aunt.*
It was in the newspaper.
We've been learning more about   *#MMIW.*

I clear my
throat.
Here's what you *need* to do,
    please:

Start talks for a
    group on Missing and Murdered Indigenous Women;

find out why there are hundreds of unsolved
    cases of #MMIW;

study why American Indian
    women and girls
        are
            ten times more likely to
                                be murdered.

Well, I— How old are you?

I'm eleven
and have been
studying   #MMIW
from my community
and other
stories

                    a   c   r   o   s   s
                         our country.

I'm also old enough to have
lost my own   Auntie Bineshiinh.
I'm old enough to
know that our government leaders
          need to lead.
I'm old enough to never
want to have another
          Native family go through this.

Yes, Ariel, yes,
I would very much
like to
visit you
and your community again.
We have so much to learn.

Miigwech, Representative.

And, Ariel,
I hear you.
And want to help.

I feel seen *and* heard.

SURVIVE?
Ariel

No, I'll
do
more
than
that.

I
will

                  thrive.

And I
will
work
hard
to
make
sure
all
Native
women and girls

                  stay safe.

Little Misko
asks again,
arms reaching
for
    m
       e.

Play?
Peekaboo!
I see . . .
YOU!

Why . . .
How . . .
did . . .
I
not . . .
see
this?
My baby brother,
little Misko,
little Miskogwan.

Miskogwan,
red
in Ojibwe.
Miskogwan = red.

Red, the color
the spirits
can see.

Like the
red dress.
Red,

red, like the
birds who danced.

And he,
little
Misko,
looking at me,
asking me
to
be
with
him,
saw
me
all along.

Mama said
I could take
my savings

from under
the bed.
We, my family and I, walk
to the
hardware
store.
We asked our community
to help buy
new bird feeders
and another
bench
and put them
right outside
the building.
    So we all can watch
    out for Tomah.

He doesn't need to
do it alone
    anymore.
He has all
of us
    now.
And so
    do I.

Everyone watched, and then
the
    birds
        danced.

SURVIVE AND BREATHE
Tomah

Survive, just   breathe.

Walk
   step
      by
         step
           up
              the
                 stage.

Hello, hello, all!
Thank you, dancers, drummers, singers, and community
members.
My name is Tomah.

clap
clap
clapclapclap

But remember, I'm only on *loan* from
the great Fort Peck Nation.
So, don't fall in love with me too much.

Ayy, Tomah!
   Go, Tomah!
         Ha ha ha!

I'm here to read something I wrote.
But first,
just know
I—
IHidThatICouldn'tReadWellForYears.

I'm telling
you all
this so
you know
it's okay
to ask for help.
Or
help
someone
who
needs it.
Help for
your heart or head.

Our ancestors
always
helped each other.

The birds always help each other.
Feathers, together, can fly.
We've forgotten that, I think.

So, here we go.
It's a poem I wrote,
and it's short.
Total opposite of me, guys!

As I look out
at you all,
into your
spirit,

I see each ancestor's
light
breathing
life
into
our
Native hearts.

We

must,

we   will

survive.

clap   *clap*   *clap*
Miigwech, Tomah!
Way to go!

I walk down from the stage.

Look! Just there in the tree.
See
how
the
brown
mama
cardinal
survives?

She
looks
like
she's

                                     invisible.

But
really
it's
how
she
survives

the
bad
things
that
could
happen.

Maybe
that's like
me.

I know
I'm not

                                        invisible

now.
Now I don't
have to
hide
behind
jokes and laughter.

I think
maybe
when
I marched

with the

                                                red dress,

I was seen,
since
I
helped
to make
    the invisible

visible.

The morning after
the spring powwow, I
sit
on my
new bench,
looking
at the
new
bird feeders.
And I
will
stay
here,

with
my
big heart,
watching
    it all.

Daddy
stops
by
my
bench
before work.
    Tomah, I . . .
    I want to tell you something.
    I know now that you are
    trying so hard at school, and
    I'm sorry for thinking otherwise.

I look at
Daddy,
but I
can't read
his eyes this
time.

Son, I go to work
protecting the
state building.
But you,
you *protect*
our Native stories.
I'm so proud of you, son.

And I
can read
his heart
in his eyes.

TOGETHER, IN COMMUNITY WE SAY
Ariel and Tomah

I see each ancestor's
    light
    breathing
life
into
our
    Native hearts.

We
        will,

we
                must

                    survive.

OJIBWE GLOSSARY

Aaniin (ah-NEEN):   greetings, hello
Biboon (be-BOON):   winter
Biindigaw (BIN-di-gaw):   enter, come in
Bineshiinh (bi-NAY-shee): bird
Bineshiiyag (bi-NEE-she-yag): birds
Dagwaagin (du-GWAH-gin):   autumn
Eya (ee-YEH):   yes
Miigwech (mee-GWECH):   thank you
Misko (mis-KO):   red
Ziigwan (ZEE-gwen):   spring (season)

AUTHOR'S NOTE

My first teaching job was in an urban Native American housing complex. The children and teens I met were so kind and
creative and welcomed me right away. The stories and lives
of the kids have stayed with me for decades now. Because of
this, I wanted to write about amazing Native kids who live in
an urban setting, who interact with each other and with their
city. So many non-Native people think most of us are on a
reservation, when in reality, the majority of us live off our
reservation lands. All people need community, and a Native
American housing complex, with many buildings, can be a
small place to call "home" in a big city.

To the urban Native kids—you have your own special
experiences, and most importantly, I hope you see yourself in
these pages set in the city. I want you to know how much I
value your stories.

To all kids—I see how you are smart in so many ways,
and not only in school subjects. Each of us has a gift, and it's
your amazing job to figure out yours!

To the Native kids who have lost someone—I hope the
birds offer you comfort as you navigate your loss and sadness.
I hope the flight of the birds reminds you to fly and soar in
your life to continue your own journey, while always remembering the ones who've walked on.

MISSING AND MURDERED INDIGENOUS WOMEN (#MMIW)

The empty red dress is a symbol of the heartbreaking crisis of our missing Native women and girls. My heart hurts for anyone who has lost someone to this tragedy. As I write this book, there is an ever-growing influential group of Native women who are gaining leadership positions in the government. These leaders and activists are advocating for our missing Native people. Native leaders in politics are among those working to keep our Native people safe. All of us can advocate, too.

As I write this today, Native women and girls are ten times more likely to be murdered than the US national average. It is a crisis that needs laws and resources to address the over five hundred missing US Native women.

Creating art can help in times of great sadness.

Jaime Black, Anishinaabe and Finnish, created the "Red Dress" art installation project, which centers on this crisis. Empty red dresses represent and honor these missing and murdered women and two-spirit people.

When I am confused, scared, and sad, I always look to nature to help me understand things. I take time to pay attention to animals and birds: how they react to the changes in seasons, how they live together in small spaces, how they are mostly silent in the darkness yet sing again at sunrise.

They, and you, will bring light to our Native communities by continuing to remember there is hope. Winter will come, yet spring is a promise we can always look to for a renewal of life. I hope you can discover, and share, your own ways of finding hope and light.

JINGLE DRESS DANCING

Jingle dancing is a form of dance at a powwow. The jingle dress is a type of regalia, or apparel, and has rows of jingles, or metal cones, attached by ribbons. The metal cones make the "jingle" sound as the person dances. There are 365 jingles sewn on a dress—the same number as days in a year. Some dancers carry a feathered fan and hold it high during certain parts of the drum song as a way to heal.

According to our traditional Ojibwe stories, this dance and dress came to a Mille Lacs Ojibwe (Minnesota) man in a dream in the early 1900s. His daughter was very sick, and in the dream this man was told to make a jingle dress for her and have her dance as a way to heal her—and it did. Dr. Brenda Child (Red Lake Ojibwe) studied the history of the jingle dress and suggests that it appeared roughly around 1920. She asked, "What happened then, and why was a new way of healing needed?" This was a period when the Spanish flu (1918–1920), a pandemic, caused people around the world to become ill, and many died.

Women in Native communities have always had the role of healers, and the jingle dress dance is another way to embrace this traditional value.

ACKNOWLEDGMENTS

A huge hug and my thanks to my Heartdrum editor, Rosemary Brosnan, and Heartdrum author-curator, Cynthia Leitich Smith. You, along with my agent, Erin Murphy, have listened to my stories and helped get them into readers' hands. Chi miigwech. Many thanks.

Also, thank you to the amazing team at Heartdrum, who made this story even better by helping to edit all my words. This book is better because of all your insight.

Chi miigwech to the amazing cover artist, Carla Joseph. You brought to life my words in your art.

I wrote this during the COVID-19 lockdown and want to send my deepest light to all those we lost. Nothing was in my control during those months, just like in your life. The only thing I could control was writing this story.

To my family, who supported me while I was writing this, for lifting up poetry to tell a complicated story.

To my writing community, without you I would not have dreamed of creating this novel in verse.

Lastly, I want to thank the #MMIW groups and everyone who works to bring home all our Native sisters.

A NOTE FROM CYNTHIA LEITICH SMITH, AUTHOR-CURATOR OF HEARTDRUM

Dear Reader,

Stories are good medicine—both fictional (or made-up) stories like this one and true stories like those tucked in your fondest memories. Yet stories aren't the *only* medicine. There's also the kind we receive from healers, the kind we find in meditation or prayer, and the kind that flows between us and those we care about.

I'm grateful that we have so many sources of good medicine. Like Tomah and Ariel, all of us face challenges, emergencies, and even crises such as the one centered on Native women like Ariel's beloved auntie. Sometimes life is painful. We feel confusion or disappointment . . . longing or grief . . . frustration or anger. We feel as though we're alone or that no one understands. We feel as though our hearts are breaking.

Your heart is strong. You understand that there is more than one way to read and to dance, to mourn and to mend. You understand that not everyone has the same amount of wealth or gets the same amount of help when they need it most. You care, and that makes a difference for the better. Hope rises when we open our hearts.

Have you read many stories by and about Indigenous people? I hope *Red Bird Danced* inspires you to read more.

The novel is published by Heartdrum, a Native-focused imprint of HarperCollins Children's Books, which offers stories about young Native heroes by Indigenous authors and illustrators. I love that author Dawn Quigley wrote this book in verse. Her thoughtful poetry beckons and confides while offering us space to breathe and reflect on this tender story.

Mvto,
Cynthia Leitich Smith

In 2014, We Need Diverse Books (WNDB) began as a simple hashtag on Twitter. The social media campaign soon grew into a 501(c)(3) nonprofit with a team that spans the globe. WNDB is supported by a network of writers, illustrators, agents, editors, teachers, librarians, and book lovers, all united under the same goal—to create a world where every child can see themselves in the pages of a book. You can learn more about WNDB programs at www.diversebooks.org.

DAWN QUIGLEY

is a citizen of the Turtle Mountain Band of Ojibwe, North Dakota. All of her books in the Jo Jo Makoons series, *Jo Jo Makoons: The Used-to-Be Best Friend, Jo Jo Makoons: Fancy Pants,* and *Jo Jo Makoons: Snow Day,* as well as her debut YA novel, *Apple in the Middle,* were awarded American Indian Youth Literature Honors. She is a PhD education university faculty member and a former K–12 reading and English teacher as well as an Indian Education program codirector. She lives in the Minneapolis, Minnesota, area. You can find her online at dawnquigley.com.

CYNTHIA LEITICH SMITH

is the bestselling, acclaimed author of books for all ages, including *Rain Is Not My Indian Name, Indian Shoes, Jingle Dancer, Sisters of the Neversea,* and *Hearts Unbroken,* which won the American Indian Youth Literature Award; she is also the anthologist of *Ancestor Approved: Intertribal Stories for Kids.* Most recently, she was named the 2021 NSK Neustadt Laureate. Cynthia is the author-curator of Heartdrum, a Native-focused imprint at HarperCollins Children's Books, and serves as the Katherine Paterson Endowed Chair on the faculty of the MFA program in writing for children and young adults at Vermont College of Fine Arts. She is a citizen of the Muscogee Nation and lives in Austin, Texas. You can visit Cynthia online at cynthialeitichsmith.com.